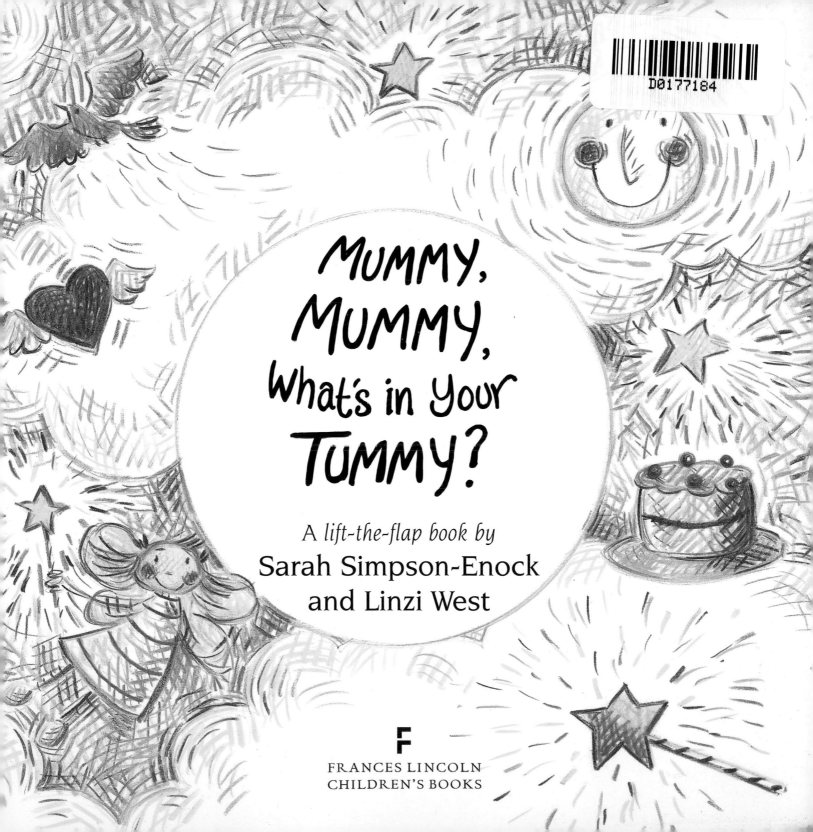

Mummy, Mummy, What's in Your Tummy?

A lift-the-flap book by

Sarah Simpson-Enock
and Linzi West

F

FRANCES LINCOLN
CHILDREN'S BOOKS

Oh,
Mummy,
Mummy,
what's in your
tummy?

We do want
to know
what's making
it grow.

A fairy
with
wings?

A boat
painted
blue?

The Man in the Moon?

A pink
birthday
cake?

A round,
red
balloon?

A **big**, yellow sun?

Just
what will
it be?

It's our
new
baby!

First published in Great Britain in 2008 and in the USA in 2009 by
Frances Lincoln Children's Books, 4 Torriano Mews,
Torriano Avenue, London NW5 2RZ

First paperback published in 2009

www.franceslincoln.com

British Library Cataloguing in Publication Data
available on request

ISBN: 978-1-84780-068-8

Printed in Heshan, Guangdong, China by Leo Paper Products Ltd.
in December 2009

3 5 7 9 8 6 4 2

MORE TITLES ILLUSTRATED BY LINZI WEST
FROM FRANCES LINCOLN CHILDREN'S BOOKS

Linzi West

Two delightful first concept board books looking at colour and sensations in sunny seaside setting.

A Beach Ball Has Them All

Green, red, blue
and many more.
Learn the colours
and spot them all!

Warm Sun, Soft Sand

Soft, squidgy sand
and nice warm sun.
Come to the beach
and have some fun!

Frances Lincoln titles are available from all good bookshops.
You can also buy books and find out more about your favourite titles, authors and illustrators
on our website: www.franceslincoln.com